THE GOAT PARADE

by Steven Kroll
pictures by
Tim Kirk

Parents Magazine Press • New York

Library of Congress Cataloging in Publication Data.
Kroll, Steven. The goat parade.
Summary: A young boy finds himself inadvertently leading an
extraordinary parade of goats into his school.
[1. Stories in rhyme.   2. Goats—Fiction]
I. Kirk, Tim, ill.   II. Title.
PZ8.3.K899G0   1983   [E]   82-10604
ISBN 0-8193-1099-9   AACR2
ISBN 0-8193-1100-6 (lib. bdg.)

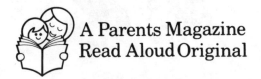

A Parents Magazine
Read Aloud Original

For Stephanie Calmenson,
who got her goats —S.K.

For Mom and Dad —T.K.

Once a year
At ten to nine
Many goats
Jump into line.

Not a one
Can be delayed
Time to join
The goat parade!

Goats with wings
Goats on springs

Goats seen wearing
Diamond rings.

Goats in coats
Goats in boats
Goats attached to
Giant floats.

Goats with ties
Goats with pies
Goats of every
Shape and size.

Up and down
And through the streets
You can hear
Their noisy bleats.

Here and there
And 'round the town
You won't see
A single frown.

Hold on now
Things could get strange—
Coming close
To hearing range

Is a boy
Named Sammy Pike
And he's on
His two-wheel bike.

Pedaling hard
The ride is great
School's ahead
Sam can't be late.

Straight into
The goats he rides
Nicking horns
And bumping hides.

Goats complain
And make a fuss
Sammy's like
A great big bus.

Plowing through
He gets ahead
And the goats
Like being led.

So each one
Against the rule

Follows Sam
Right into school.

Then they're at
His classroom door

What, you ask,
Is now in store?

Sammy knocks
And steps inside
Boys and girls
Run off and hide

Under desks
And under coats
Who has seen
So many goats?

Goats on desks
And goats on chairs
Goats are backed
Up to the stairs.

Goats on sills
And goats in sinks
Who knows what
The teacher thinks?

Now our Sam
Knows he can't bluff
Time to show
He's got the stuff.

He gets out
His megaphone
Tells the goats
"You must go home!"

They line up
Just like before
And he leads
Them out the door.

Down the stairs
And through the streets
Once again
You hear their bleats.

But the noise
Soon starts to fade
Tired goats
Are seeking shade.

Time to rest
And time to feed
Leafy trees
Are what they need.

Back at school
Sam gets a cheer
Just the words
He wants to hear.

"You're the best!"
And "We're for you!"
"We knew you'd
Know what to do!"

But there's more
It's not the end
Can you guess
What's 'round the bend?

Next year when
The time comes 'round
Boys and girls
Without a sound

All get up
And leave their chairs
Boys and girls
Go down the stairs.

Off they go
They won't be swayed
Off to lead . . .

The goat parade.

About the Author

STEVEN KROLL explains how he got started writing THE GOAT PARADE: "I had just come from a meeting with a special person, my editor at Parents, Stephanie Calmenson. During the meeting we talked about goats. Suddenly, as I walked downtown, goats were everywhere: skating in the street, dancing on the rooftops, tumbling out of cars, racing through my head. Then and there I knew I would write a book about goats. But what would those goats be doing? Why, they'd be on parade, of course! And I rushed home to begin."

Steven Kroll, author of many popular books for children, including DIRTY FEET and OTTO, for Parents, lives in New York City.

About the Artist

TIM KIRK says that he liked drawing the goats most when they went into the classroom. "The goats are doing all the things I always wanted to do in school, but never had the nerve for." He thinks it would have been especially fun to play the bagpipes he brought back from Ireland. "I haven't practiced much," he says, "so I wouldn't be surprised if a goat could play better than I do."

Tim Kirk lives in Long Beach, California. He works for Walt Disney Productions designing, among other things, shows and attractions for Disneyland and Walt Disney World. He is also a five time "Hugo" award winner for his fantasy illustration.